I Love My Mommy

Sebastien Braun

HarperCollinsPublishers

My mommy watches
me while I play.

My mommy takes
me swimming.

My mommy
helps me
to climb.

My mommy stays
by my side.

My mommy
cleans me up.

My mommy
feeds me.

My mommy plays
games with me.

My mommy works
really hard.

My mommy carries
me when I am tired.

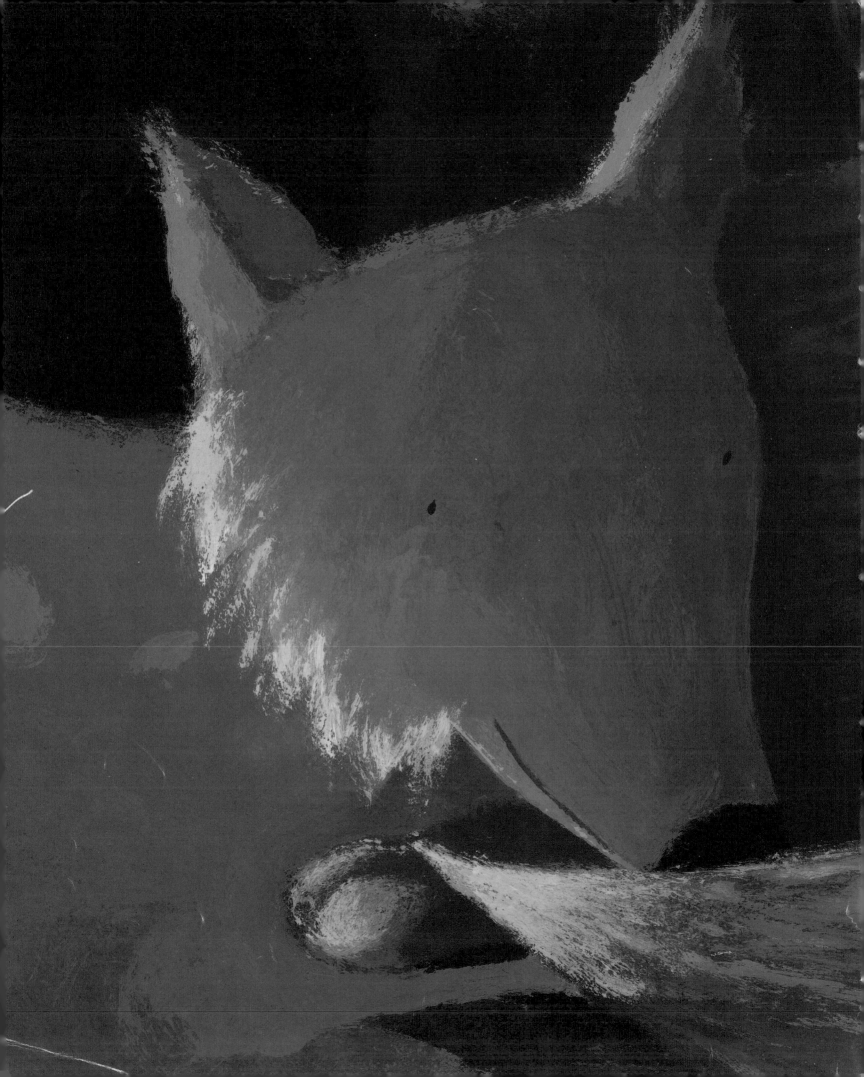

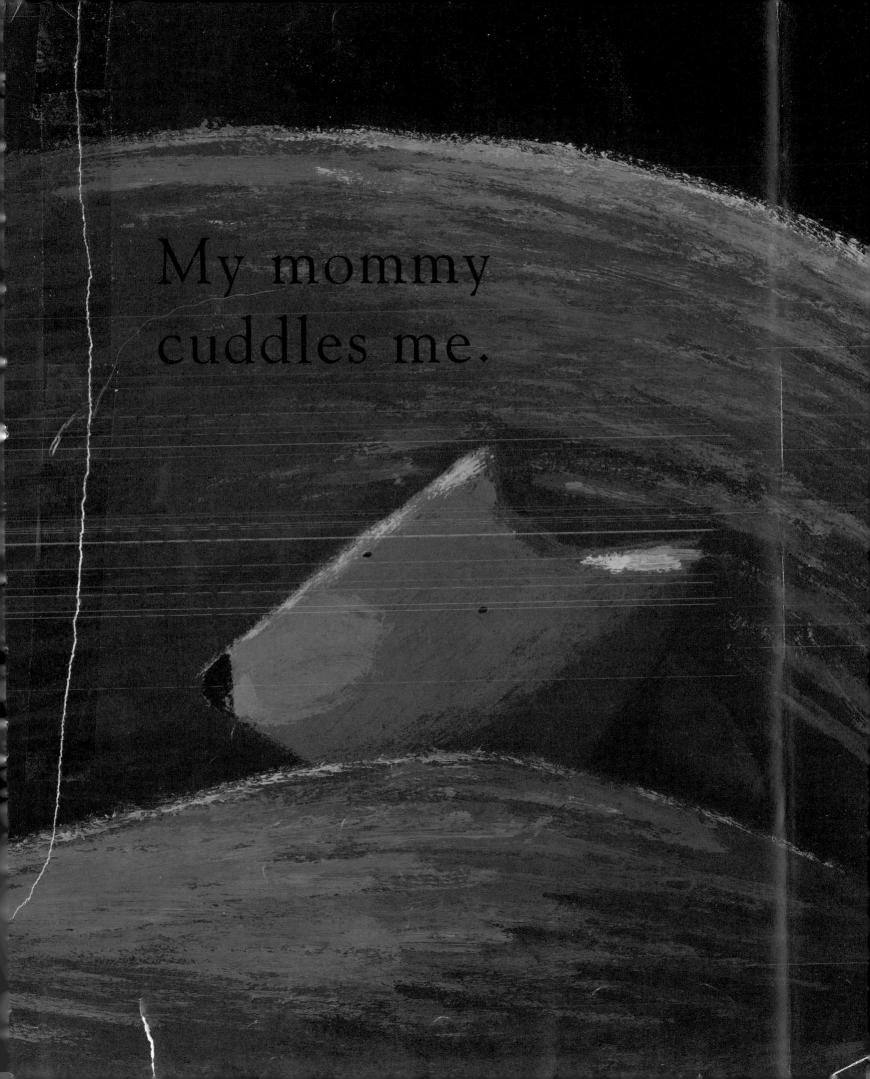

My mommy
cuddles me.

My mommy is always
there for me.

I love my mommy.